REBIRTH SAGA

REBIRTH

DRACO SPENCER

Want to read more exciting stories for **FREE?**

Join my V.I.P List now!

I regularly GIVEAWAY FREE books and SPECIAL DISCOUNTS!

Join my mailing list and be one of thousands we already receiving FREEBIES!

Join by visiting this site:

http://www.ravenspress.com/infinitedreamspubbonus/

Or Scan this QR Code from your smartphone to go the website directly

INFINITE DREAMS
PUBLISHING

ISBN-13: 978-1523889877

ISBN-10: 152388987X

http://www.ravenspress.com/infinitedreamspubbonus/

TABLE OF CONTENTS

PROLOGUE

The old Datsun glided through the graveyard like an angel of death. Its driver was a 36-year-old woman with long blonde hair swept back in a tight magenta bandana. The teenaged boy in the shotgun seat had his head bowed, fist pressed into his teeth. Too macho to cry, he wrestled Olympically with the tears.

"It's okay, buddy," said the lady, clapping a firm hand on his knee.

"I know." He shrugged and lifted his head, emerald eyes still tinged the color of burgundy despite his efforts.

They reached the end of the mausoleum's driveway. The boy hopped out first, and stumbled in the tan dead grass. The woman slid out a perfect bouquet of holiday colored blossoms cradled in her arms. She looked up at the ceiling of the tomb and cracked an elated smile.

"Check it, Alex! They put up lights!" Her voice was hushed, enraptured.

The tiny white Christmas light bulbs twinkled like a wink from the angels.

Alex sniffed, unable to force a laugh. With a shrug, he stumbled into the dim tomb. He didn't look up as he ambled along. He'd memorized the path to his best friend's marble plaque.

His heart stopped when he did at last look up.

"Renee!" His voice cracked. Vibrations of his piercing shriek echoed off the marble and glass-packed walls.

Renee flew to his side, face the color of an ashtray. Her eyes turned to globes when she saw what he had.

A marble plaque that read "Nicolas Avalon 1998-2015" was lying on its side against the wall.

"Oh God!" Renee sank to her knees, chewing her thumb to choke down vomit.

The tomb had been broken into.

* * *

The Durango Police Department flocked to the scene. The whole mausoleum was shrouded in yellow caution tape. Despite a rookie cop's insistence, Renee and Alex were unwilling to leave.

"He was family! Sort of..." Renee thrashed as officers tried to force her from the scene.

"You're the foster home facilitator, right?" Police Chief Riggs grabbed the young officer by the shoulder, prompting her to wait.

"That's right. Renee Vierra." She tossed her head defiantly.

"Okay, she can stay."

"The kid stays too. The boy they've grave robbed was his best friend." Renee jutted out her chin, outraged. Alex stooped on the icy floor, lips turned purple more from shock than cold. The cop released Renee and she swooped to the kid, knelt beside him and protectively wrapped him in her arms.

"It's okay, Alex."

The forensic researchers arrived. Their voices were hushed as they peered into the tomb. Alex dug his fingers into the concrete floor until blood dripped from his nail beds. Renee gripped his shoulder to steady him. One of the forensics slid the coffin onto the floor. They were just checking for damage to it. Was this a robbery or a simple grave desecration? Who would want to desecrate the tomb of a 17-year-old boy?

The coffin's lid flapped loose on its hinges. They eased it open, with suspicious glances at Renee and Alex. The kid started to hyperventilate, despite all attempts to look chill.

Silence pervaded. They stared into the coffin truly perplexed. It was empty.

Forensic Officer Braxton's face transformed to alabaster. He traced his finger along the lid of the coffin, eyes growing wider by the second. He took a cotton swab to the lace that lined the bottom and came away with blood.

"The lid was pried loose by the toe of a male's size 10 shoe driven into it. There are scratches that have traces of fingernail in the lid. The blood on the lace dripped from one of the gashes in the coffin's ceiling. It's 48 hours old tops."

The Police Chief pushed his way forward.

"What the heck are you suggesting, Braxton?"

Braxton swallowed and looked apologetically at Renee and Alex.

"This coffin, sir, was broken open from the inside." Braxton's lips had turned blue.

"Sir, that's a load of bull. The coroner's report for Nicolas Avalon just pulled up in the computer. The kid got iced in a hit and run 7 months ago." An officer spat, thoroughly disgusted.

"Want proof, Rogers? Get me DNA samples!" Braxton's menacing eyes flashed. His ferocity told them that this was not a joke or even incompetence.

They slipped the droplet into a card and plugged it into the computer. Behold! A faded black and white photo of Nicolas appeared on the computer screen.

"My God!" The Police Chief's knees began to knock together.

Rogers blanched.

"So, this means..." She wrapped her mouth in a shaking palm.

"Nicolas Avalon broke out of his tomb not more than 48 hours ago." Braxton finished for her.

"Impossible!" said Officer Dawes.

"Look around you! What else do you need, a neon sign?! Lazarus has come forth, ladies and gentlemen. How and why? That's what we got to figure out. Everybody head back to the station. Double time." Chief Riggs snapped his fingers, herding the spectators away from the scene.

CHAPTER 1

The emerald 69' Mustang Mach 1 rolled into Durango down main-street. It was headed for Santa Bianca's Children's Home right outside the city limits.

The Colorado dust swamped the sky. Like this were their Damascus road, the officers were blinded by the dust grit and were deafened by the roar of her engine.

She flounced out of the cab. Her pumps dug into the dust. The tails of her leather trench coat caught in the winter's gale and blew up to reveal her tie-dye skinny jeans. John Lennon-style shades veiled her eyes.

Marilyn Avalon studied the lot of them, hands folded behind her back like a drill sergeant. They all waited for her to say 'at ease', but she never uttered the command. With a toss of her pinned-up dirt blonde hair, she did an about-face, headed for the porch.

"Is Renee Vierra where I can speak with her?" she asked the depressed blonde who leaned over the rails, a bottle of Coca-Cola pressed to her lips.

The blonde looked up and squared her jaw.

"You're looking at her?"

"Hello, Ms. Vierra. We spoke on the phone?" Marilyn smiled.

"Right. You're the missing person's private detective Dr. Swift was talking about." Renee nodded, relieved to see her.

"Heard you've got a kid on the loose?"

"Ha! Yeah, that's an understatement. Nicky's a good kid, never hurt a fly, but he's always been a bit of a handful. Likes to slip out the backdoor and hustle pool after curfew. Never thought I'd see the day when he'd break out of his own...His own umm...Well, his grave, ma'am."

Avalon wondered if this might be a bad lip read.

"His grave?"

Renee laughed.

"No, you heard right. Thought it'd be easier to break that part to you in person. Nicky...He got killed about 7 months ago walking home from school. It was a hit and run. Police were calling it a vehicular homicide." She shrugged and took a shaky breath.

"Going on 72 hours ago, he...The forensics seem to think he...uhh...Broke out. Like out of his coffin and the mausoleum we had him entombed in."

Marilyn plucked her shades from her face, jaw dropped.

"You mean, like your garden variety Lazarus?"

"I had a hard time with it too, trust me. Losing him-Well, all of these kids are like my own, you know? You get attached to them. None more than Nicky. Honestly, I was in no frame of mind to hire you. No offense. But it's gospel. The pediatrician that looks after all my wards recommended you."

As if summoned, a tall, slender ginger appeared on the porch hands clasped in front of him, teeth set on edge.

"A word, Renee?"

"Sure. Go ahead."

"It's just, I'm worried about Alex. Think he might be bordering on catatonic. I'd like to have him committed until this all blows over." The pediatrician smiled, knowing what he was saying sounded horrible.

"Oh God, no! He'll kill me if I put him in the Psych Ward!" Renee gulped like she was trying to swallow a Globe.

"There's no shame in it. Only for a few days?"

"Dr. Swift, I appreciate your concern. It's just...I need my boy to be with me, okay?"

Swift held up a hand in mock surrender, a placid smile spread across his face.

"Understood. But he's bad off. I'd go so far as to say cracked, at least 'til further notice. Rest him up, understand? Oh, and if Nicolas shows around sooner than later, ease Alex into it, alright?"

"You got it!" Renee broke out in nervous giggles.

"Odd this. I'd bet my Grandad's last dollar this is probably Lazarus Syndrome. Almost unheard of, and certainly never heard of after this long. Still is the only explanation I can figure." Dr. Swift clutched his chin, eyes far off with trouble.

"Lazarus syndrome?" said Marilyn. She wondered if there was a medical term for 'everything and the kitchen sink'.

The Doctor's eyes lit up with ecstasy.

"Oh, hello, you must be Detective Avalon! I've always wanted to meet you. Huge fan of your blog!" He rushed to her and shook both her hands.

"Ah, well thanks. I wondered who those 3 readers were."

They all laughed. Dr. Swift shrugged.

"I might be one of few, but I'm a devoted minority, Detective."

"Please. Call me Marilyn."

"Marilyn, then." Swift was blushing. Marilyn found it to be adorable.

"You must be the patron saint of Durango? Except with that accent, I'd say you're from West London." Marilyn winked.

"Highest marks! But God no! I'm merely the doctor for the kids here. Lucas Swift. It's truly an honor, Detective. I mean, Marilyn."

She laughed and shook her head.

"What's Lazarus Syndrome, Doctor?"

"Well, simply put, it's when an inanimate person becomes vital on their own after all attempts at reviving them have been stopped. It usually only occurs in subjects that have been clinically dead for a few minutes. There have been a few cases of it happening days after the death, though. Still, it's never been recorded as happening half a year after the subject expired. Long shot, I know. It's my best guess either way."

"Your guess is as good as mine here. I rest my case." Marilyn hung her head in a mock pout.

"Not so fast. My boy's out there traipsing through Wild Country. You're the best bloodhound we've got on the job. Don't let me down." Renee smiled, happy for the first time in months. She motioned for Marilyn to follow her and lead her into the house.

* * *

In the center of the novel farmhouse, Chief Riggs sat in front of a squirming teenage girl. She popped gum loudly and rolled her smoky mascara-caked eyes.

"Look! I don't know anything! That nerd died like ages ago. No one cares where he's spooked off to!" She whined, drumming her fingers against her thighs.

"Well, I'd start caring if I were you, little miss. Because I've got to find him and I need your full co-operation." Chief Riggs was rubbing his eyelids in exhaustion.

"Why don't you ask his bestie?" She tossed her head with a snarky snicker and blew a bubble that burst obnoxiously.

"Wait, I forgot. That nerd's not talking period. My bad!" She covered her pursed lips with her palm.

"Listen real careful like, doll face. I'd love to let you sit time out in the county jail until mold started growing off the bottom of your lips, but even I admit that's a bit extreme. It's really a simple question and when you've answered it you can go back to spray netting your freaky hair. Did you or did you not know Nicolas Avalon?"

Marilyn stopped in the hallway. She made a mental note that the missing boy had the same surname as she did. Good, it would be easy to remember.

"Sally! Straighten up for the Chief or you're on bovine enema duty for the next 5 months!" Renee snapped her fingers.

"Oh God! Yes, officer. Yes, I totally knew Nick. Heck, everybody did. He's...Uh, he was, like the valedictorian of our class up until the day he got made into roadkill." Sally threw her hands up in surrender.

"Alright, now we're getting somewhere. I'm taking that means you knew about some of his hang out places. For starters, where do you think he'd go after freshly busting out of his tomb? Where does Nicky Avalon go to kick it when he's cold, hungry, and casket sharp? " Chief Riggs leaned over his knees in renewed interest.

"Like I'd know? Seriously, you should ask Alex."

"Where's Alex, then? I'll ask him." Marilyn stepped forward.

"Huh. Good luck. He's turned into a robot." Sally rolled her eyes.

"Just tell me where he is?" Marilyn folded her arms.

"Ah, so you're the private investigator, eh? The Calvary has arrived and praise the Lord. Kudos to you if you can get the kid to speak. He's upstairs, facing Mecca." The Chief indicated with his head.

Marilyn took to the creaky staircase. The shadows fell long across the upstairs rooms, reflecting the sadness that had come to the foster home. Although she hadn't known him, Marilyn could feel Nicolas' absence. Apparently, in their own way, so did everyone. The kids smiled shyly at her as she passed down the lengthy hallway that ran between the east and west wings of the house.

"Hey. Alex's room?" Marilyn stopped a tall boy in a football jersey.

"Which Alex, ma'am? There's like 3?"

Marilyn swallowed.

"Nicolas Avalon's friend?"

The boy's eyes lit up.

"Prescott...Okay, yeah, you must be the sleuth chick Papa Vierra said was coming. Well, Alex can't come to the phone right now. He's...uh...wasted. Been staring out the east wing window for 12 hours, no joke. Just staring, stoned. Seeing Nicky's box...He's messed up."

Marilyn felt the weight of this situation drive home. She nodded, shaking off the dust from the yard and the chill of dread that ran up her spine.

"All the same. Whatever freaky thing is aligning up in Space made this happen beats me. Nicky's clearly not resting in peace. I need Alex to help me put a ghost to bed."

The boy shrugged.

"Cool, I guess. I'll take you to him."

Of all the rooms in the dim farmhouse, Alex Prescott's was the darkest. He sat with the shadows draped around him like fabric, forehead pressed against the frosted glass of the massive window beside his bed.

"Yo, Prescott! The sleuth chick's here. Wants to talk to you!"

Alex didn't move.

"Yeah, see, I told you. Hey, if you need something later, I'm Brandon." The boy shrugged and left Marilyn alone in the dusky room.

"Hey, Alex." She stepped closer, making a floorboard squeak.

To her surprise, Alex finally did look up. She stood transfixed. His fine-boned face was pinched like it would shatter into a thousand shards of porcelain. He clenched his teeth and his purple lips quivered spasmodically. His emerald eyes glowered with bloodshot veins. The spiked-bangs hairstyle he was sporting couldn't hide the patches he ripped out of his scalp. These oozed blood like scarlet sideburns down the edges of his face. He had one of his fists pressed to the window pane. The knuckles were bloody. He'd chewed them to the bone.

A mess? What a severe understatement! Alex Prescott looked like Nagasaki after the bomb.

Marilyn held her breath. She went and embraced him out of instinct. He flinched but didn't resist her.

She eased up off of him and took his face in her hands.

"We can get him back." She peered down into his eyes, breath bated.

Trembling, he eased himself up tall and plucked his iPhone from his jeans' pocket.

"He texted me." Alex closed his eyes, hoarse and dizzy.

Marilyn took the phone, in shaking fingers. Silently she read:

"Alex, it's Nick. New phone. It's freaky, man. I blacked out and now I can't remember much of what happened. Seriously, though, watch your back. There are people following me. I think I'm in trouble. Which if I'm in trouble, then you probably are too. Creeps usually go after family and friends, right? I'm going to head for 'Castle Coyote' from when we were kids. I'm not saying that you should come after me. I just wanted you to know that I'm okay. You're probably freaked! Dude, I'm sorry."

"Nicky...Nicky's dead? Now he's texting-Oh God!" Alex pressed his face against his knees.

"Can you take me to the place he's talking about?"

Alex gave a reluctant nod.

CHAPTER 2

He ran blind. His head hurt, which was his sole focus. Agonizing migraines had been plaguing him for going on three days now.

There were voices in the woods.

"It'll be a lot easier if you stop making it hard."

"Doesn't have to be like this, kiddo."

"Come back, Nicky! Let's not make this so hard!"

Nick felt his stomach knit itself up into a tight fist of fear. He threw his head back, hoping maybe this would give him an extra ounce of speed.

Durango isn't known for extremely cold winters, but winter it was. The grass was slick with frost.

He slipped and rolled downhill. He heard a few of his ribs crack, but barely noticed the pain.

All he could think about was the voices. The sound of feet chasing him under the shadows of the trees. Dogs barking. He thought maybe he even heard a truck meander through the foilage.

He landed on his knees and felt blood pool around his knuckles.

This might not be so scary if he could just remember why it was happening.

He remembered blacking out. He could almost see it happen. He was walking down the side of main-street, heading back from school. There was a sound behind him like somebody punching the gas. His neck had snapped in the direction of the noise. A truck was swiveling like a crazy snake down the lane closest to him.

He remembered heavy force and going numb from the impact. He'd flown through the air and landed in a puddle of his own blood and intense pain. It had started to go dark and he heard Alex screaming his name.

Oh God, Alex had been there!

Was he okay?

The voices were getting closer.

Why couldn't he remember anything? He felt like he'd been out for centuries.

There was nothing before the car crash. His entire life was distant watercolors.

He leaped up and ran. That's all he could think to do. Ran as his eyes teared up from the pain in his head. Good God, what the heck was happening?

He was elated when he saw the old tree fort. He and Alex had built it on an outing the first year they'd lived with the Santa Bianca kids. It was a landmark of childhood and safety to Nick. Innocence and a place to crash is what the confused teen needed now.

He dove like a baseball player and slid for home. The feet rushed past him. His head came up abruptly on the hard trunk of the ancient hollow cedar.

The impact jarred his memory. Not enough to solve his current dilemma, but enough to answer his most nagging question.

"I died." He blurted to the darkness.

He was smothering in the blows of a full-blown panic attack then. There was no one here to help him back either. His legs kicked out and stirred up the cedar needles. He dug his fists into the ground and tore at moss. In a daze, he tried to slow his hyperventilating and think this through. It was getting the better of him.

"I didn't just die. I was murdered. But why?"

He didn't have time to work that out. The dogs were coming back. They wouldn't need to see him. They could sniff him out.

"Think, dude! Got to get out of the basic trajectory of evil!"

He started crawling forward on his belly USMC fashion.

* * *

The Mach 1 peeled off down the main highway. The sun looked down from the sloping blue arches that wreathed Durango in majesty. Renee Vierra was sitting in the shotgun seat. Alex Prescott lay in the back. His eyes floated around the cab and he almost smiled.

"Kiddo, you sure you're okay to be doing this? The Doc wanted me to rest you up." Renee's brow crumbled in concern.

Alex had a blank expression as he stared at the scrawling red and dirty blues of the Colorado roadside. He shrugged, running a hand over his tender head. Marilyn winced as she looked at him in the rearview mirror. It had to have been agonizing. What kind of internal darkness had compelled him to tear his hair out?

"I'm not going to be okay until Nick's back home and totally safe." He shrugged, twisting his mouth in a white bunch.

Renee nodded.

"You're saying he's gone to our old camp-sight?"

"It's like a mile away from there as the crow flies. We marked the way by carving pictures on the trees around it. It was like a code alphabet to our clubhouse. Hey, quit smiling like that! We were 12 and 12 ½ !" Alex narrowed his eyes as Renee stifled an endeared giggle.

The riffs to "Black Hole Sun" interrupted the moment. It was Alex's ringtone.

"Oh God…" He chewed his fingernails reluctant to look. Marilyn drew a heavy breath.

"Hey! I know all of this is freaky, but it's still Nicky, right? He clearly hasn't figured out what's happened yet. When he does, it's going to wig him out just as much as it has you. This doesn't have to be an American Horror Story. This is a golden opportunity, my young friend. There is hardly a soul alive that has gotten a loved one back from the dead." She forced a smile.

Alex gaped. It hadn't occurred to him until she'd said it. He plucked the phone from his pocket again, braced for whatever the screen portended.

"Alex. It's Nick. Dude, you were at the scene of my accident. Are you okay?

This is messed up, bro. I have no idea how it's even possible and I'm legit freaking at the moment.

I died, didn't I? I was murdered."

With a nervous gasp, Alex began to type back.

"Hey, Nick. Yeah, I'm okay. I have no idea how to do this, man. How to talk to you. Tell you this.

You've been dead for 7 months."

 "What's he saying?" Renee asked. She twisted around to look at Alex. It was a miracle, no questions asked. Regardless of the circumstances which lead here, this was more than they could have ever wished for. Nature dictated that Nicky Avalon was never to say anything again. That they could never talk to him again. He was dead. It was done.

Now they were texting him like it was any other day. As if that fateful day in the spring never even happened.

"He's starting to remember." Alex's eyes flashed as his own words registered in his ears.

This could be both a tremendously good and bad thing.

CHAPTER 3

The fish bowl blip sound echoed into the tree's dark hull. Nicky jumped. He was honestly scared out of his mind. It wasn't just the distant past he was forgetting. He had trouble remembering recent things, like how he got these new clothes. There was a tag in the sleeve of his black hoodie that said "Boot Barn". The jeans were store-bought stiff. He'd even forgotten to take the paper out of the toes of his Nikes.

"Shopping center... Uh, I sold a few cartons of cigarettes I'd stashed behind the Principle's favorite poplar for quick cash. Mrs. Thurman screamed when I walked through her yard, but I didn't think it was weird because Mrs. Thurman is batty. Then I sold that Harley I restored last summer and hid in Old Man Payne's tool shed for a lot of extra cash. I bought like 7 burgers, butt-loads of Coke and pop rocks, and a milkshake. People everywhere I went were giving me the truancy stare. It's cold out and there are Christmas lights. I'm not truant. I should be on Christmas break, right? Which means they were staring at me because I'm supposed to be dead."

He felt like bawling. He could technically get by with it too. After all, he was supposed to be dead and there wasn't anybody around for God only knew how far. He could just tune up like a little girl if he wanted to. Far too macho to sob like a baby, even in secret, he swiped at the tears that were slipping free nonetheless.

"Gah! Okay! What the heck is happening?!"

He shook his head and tried to focus. On something other than the chainsaw massacre brain ache he was experiencing between either of his temples. His fingers knotted his hair in supreme frustration and he plucked two large clumps of it free from the roots.

"Think, brainless!" He growled and kicked the wall of the hollow tree.

The fish bowl chime echoed three consecutive times. Blue light cascaded his face. It registered at last that it was coming from the phone.

Squinting, he read the tiny print.

"Calm down, pal. The Doc and Papa Vierra hired a private detective. She's smoking hot and seems to have her ducks in line. I honestly think she'll be able to help you. Not just saying it to keep you from freaking."

From what had to be lightyears away, Alex calmed the storm in him. He felt his lips twist in a tiny smirk. His fingers moved faster than his thought processes to type his reply.

"Totally calm over here. For a Zombie that's standard procedure anyway. I'm chilling in the tree fort. Tell the Gramps to put some pedal into it!"

He jabbed the "Send" button with a trembling finger and sagged into the leaves. It might actually be okay.

That notion left him instantly. He felt the slobber hit the side of his face before he heard the gurgling growl.

Nick sprung up into a spider monkey's fight stance. His hair was standing on end, all up the back of his skull and the nape of his neck. He even felt the five o'clock shadow forming around his lips prickle and scrape his nostrils.

"Okay, for real, Nicolas. Think of something!"

He was drawing nothing but blanks. Unfortunate. The dog lunged forward and bit into his shoulder. Nick screamed and tried to tear free of the dog. He leaned up and sunk his teeth desperately into its neck, thinking that would hurt it enough to free him. His bite wasn't strong enough to pierce the bulldog's hide.

"Look what I've got, boys! Bourbon! Release, boy!"

The dog's teeth came free of Nick's bones. The kid sprawled on the ground in a daze. With one hand, he tried to massage the dog bite, with the other he jabbed a finger at the figure who towered over him.

"It's fuzzy, but I know you from somewhere. Somewhere like school maybe or Santa Bianca's...Or both."

He didn't get the chance to place this mystery re-acquaintance. The butt of a rifle collided with his forehead. Darkness took him again.

* * *

"He's not answering his phone!" Alex was in a panic. It had only been 10 minutes, but 10 minutes is 10,000 years when you're talking to a loved one that died recently.

"Maybe he's just scared. You said we were almost to the old tree fort anyway, right?" Renee tried to keep her voice hopeful.

"He's gone." Marilyn's blood had gone cold as she uttered the words.

"What?" Alex looked crestfallen.

Marilyn pointed to the muddy tracks leading away.

"The leaves are too crushed for this time of the year. The wildlife doesn't venture too far from their dens when it gets this cold. Besides nothing leaves a print with grooves in it. Those are mud tires. Some off-road dually truck pulled through here less than an hour ago."

Marilyn strayed farther into the thicket.

"Look! There are dog prints too! A shoe print there, size 10. Nicky wears a 10 didn't you say?"

She followed the trail to the hollowed tree Alex had described.

"God, please...Not again." Renee's voice trembled in the air.

Alex sank to his knees and crawled forward on his hands. There in the mud and wet leaves lay a cheap burner cell with a huge hole knocked in the text screen. It had been crushed in the obvious struggle.

"Not just gone. He's been taken." Marilyn clarified. Alex bit down on the back of his fist again, head bobbing in panic.

"Taken? Where?" Renee went green around the lips.

Marilyn looked up to the body of the tree. There was a scrap of white paper pinned to it with a box cutter. Two words were scribbled across it.

"He's yours."

Marilyn blanched. She teetered on her heels and grabbed the tree. Clenched her mouth in her fist and uttered a tiny wheezing sob.

"Yeah, okay. The name makes sense now. This just got personal!" She fanned herself with her hands.

"Do not pass out!" She commanded herself in her head until those four words became a mantra.

This very scenario had haunted her for years. It was a nightmare come at last to life.

"What? What's it say? What does it mean, Marilyn?"

Renee snatched the paper from Marilyn and read it aloud.

"He's yours?" she asked and then her eyes lit up.

"Nicolas Avalon...Marilyn Avalon. Weird name. Not many people share it?" Renee looked at Alex, eyes popping.

Alex shook his head, not following.

"I had a baby out of wedlock when I was a younger woman. I was seeing a guy... We were just fooling around with each other. Didn't know he was married. When I found out about his wife who had just realized she was pregnant I ended it immediately. Wasn't fast enough apparently. A week later I realized that I was pregnant too. I ended their marriage, not even meaning to. By the time I delivered, I was too horrified by everything that had happened so I gave the baby up..." Marilyn clutched at her stomach and chewed her lip.

"So...that means that Nicky?" Renee's eyes went wide.

"Nicky is my son!" Marilyn sobbed.

CHAPTER 4

Nick woke up in the woods.

He breathed heavily out of his nose and tried to move.

That's when he realized that his ankles were chained. To concrete blocks.

"Nicolas. It's foolish to attempt to run. How many times do we have to go over this? You live and we monitor. You die and we take notes. You wake up and we start all over. Capisce? "

He held his breath and closed his eyes. It was rushing back now a mile a minute. He couldn't deal with this, but he really had no choice. Ready or not, it was happening now.

First things first. He needed to figure out where he was.

Twisting around on himself, he felt chains shaken by his legs and something heavy under his feet. Concrete blocks.

"Listen, alright! I get that this is important. Might change the fate of Humanity. I didn't sign up for this!"

There was a revving sound. A truck.

Nicky realized too quickly that he was connected by several chains to a truck. Which one of his captors had just thrown into neutral and was letting slide for Lake Nighthorse.

"Ah-oh, God!"

"You can't panic. Not now. Wanna stay alive? Think, brainless!"

It was truly unfortunate how he was drawing total blanks.

* * *

Marilyn clutched the note in a quaking hand. She paced Santa Bianca's living room floor.

"They knew he was my child, but I never told anyone about him. Not even my closest friends ever knew I was pregnant. I isolated myself from the whole world while I carried Nicolas. There was only one person that I ever told the secret and it was only because I felt it was the right thing to do. This can only mean one thing."

Renee raised her brows, trying to follow. Marilyn threw her hands in the air.

"It means they knew his father! He's the only one I ever told! Stay tracking with me."

"Alright, so who was Nicky's father?" Renee swallowed, reluctant to pick this scab.

Marilyn rolled her eyes and laughed.

"That trashy cowboy's name was Army Prescott. He had a prominent career in the 101st Airborne. I've always been a sucker for a man in uniform."

Alex sat up from where he slouched against the couch. He looked like someone had just electrocuted him.

"What's the matter, kid? You know something I don't?" Marilyn's eyes went wide.

"Wait a sec. Your name is Prescott, isn't it?"

Alex licked his lips.

"My dad's real name is Alexander Prescott. They don't call me Junior. It's just Alex because they've always called my dad Army. He- He won like a boat-load of Medals when he was in the 101st. He's even been interviewed on Good Morning, America a few times." Alex was shaking his head. His lips had turned purple.

"But my dad had a pretty nasty secret. He cheated on my mom a lot. She had been begging him for a baby. He didn't really want one. Just wanted her to shut up, I guess.

Mom told me the story something like this. There was a public service lady that Dad had wiled and charmed to(her words not mine) 'get in her pants'. This was what ended my Mom and Dad's marriage. She found out I was coming the same week she found out about the affair. She died of cancer when I was 12. I moved through the system a lot and finally got invited to live here in Santa Bianca's. It's like a charity or something so they take kids from all over…" His voice trailed off.

Marilyn sank into an armchair, stupefied.

"Nicky is your brother. You're almost exactly the same age because you have different mothers. Your father was a famous service member, which makes you something of a public figure just by association. You both made your way to a unique foster home that accepts children from all over the country because it's a charity…" She looked up at Renee who was looking at Alex in concern.

"Okay, so hang on here! This is all just spiraling a little bit out of the Universe for me!"Alex held up his hand.

His horror was perfectly founded. The boy he'd grown up with in foster care had suddenly died and left him alone, twisting in the winds of turbulent youth. Now he had resurrected and reappeared as his biological brother. The obvious victim of a demented murder scheme. It would be too much for anyone to take in right off.

"If the guys that took Nick knew that he was your kid, then they'd have to have learned that from my dad. Which means that my dad is in on whatever seriously warped thing it is that they are doing to Nick, right?" Alex sputtered and clutched at his knees to hide that they were trembling.

Marilyn nodded.

"Yes, that's the only logical explanation."

Alex opened his mouth to say something, but the words never came out.

"Guys!" Renee interrupted. Her eyes were glued to the room's ancient TV set.

It was trained to the local news.

"I'm Erin Pickler. We're live here at Lake Nighthorse where local fishermen allegedly witnessed a 17-year-old Caucasian male being dragged into the water chained to the bumper of an unmanned truck. What makes this account of eye-witness murder even more harrowing? The 17-year-old is being identified by police as Nicolas Avalon. The victim of the infamous Main Street vehicular homicide 7 months ago."

Marilyn leaped to her feet. The truck was bobbing about in the water like an apple. Police and firefighters were combing the lake with machinery. Would they find young Nicolas' body?

Durango was stricken with an epidemic of psychological insomnia from the image that appeared next. There were splashes and bubbles around the nose of the truck. A firefighter shouted and pointed at the water. Several people crowded close to the shore.

Suddenly, Nick's head cleared the surface of the water gasping for breath. His hair was clinging to his face and he spluttered. His eyes were wide with terror.

"I cut him from the crash! I took his body from the crash!" One of the firefighters was screaming hysterically and pointing at the boy.

Hysteria seems to spread infectiously. The boy made a bolt for it, swimming into the deeper water at a break-neck clip.

The camera lingered in his wake as though it had been abandoned.

Marilyn, Renee, and Alex exchanged glances.

CHAPTER 5

He jerked. It felt like he had been asleep for centuries. The frigid water jarred him to the bones. All of his muscles were pulled by the force of his thrashing into wakefulness. He could feel them tearing.

His eyes came open underwater. Blurry, greenish gray, dead worms floating about his head. Lake water.

He couldn't remember anything. Yet somehow this situation felt all too familiar. Larger than life.

His head cleared the surface. He gasped for breath out of reflex. The late afternoon light pierced into his panic-stricken mind. It was the only thing he could focus on for a split second. Light. Too much. Toxic to the delicate balance of his quaking world.

Then there were people screaming. Why were they screaming?

He felt his head spin around. He was in the middle of a lake. There were firefighters, police officers, and local news crews along the shore. Some of them were transfixed in silent terror. Some of them were pointing and screaming random things.

"I cut him from the crash! He-I'd know that face anywhere!" One of the firefighter's had collapsed to his knees in unholy terror.

Nicky bolted from an instinctual reaction. They were the predators he was the prey, so far as he was concerned. This Frankenstein's monster life was new and threatened. He had to make tracks and fast.

It was an auditory hallucination. Hysteric en-route, Nicky didn't know that. He could hear their voices in his mind. The people that had done this to him.

"Hyperkalemia, Nicolas. It means too much potassium in the blood. You know the nutrient in bananas. For most people it's a disease. It causes irregularities in heart rhythms. You remember, we've talked about it, that's what we call arrhythmia. You and your family, however, seem to have a highly unique irregularity in your gene pool. You appear to have scheduled hyperkalemia. It's almost like clockwork, but your blood seems to trigger bouts of the imbalance at sporadic intervals, as though it were making an excess to use for some purpose..."

Nick tried to block the voice out. It was impossible to stuff his ears when he was treading water. He could do nothing but grit his teeth and listen to this schizophrenic monolog.

"Nicolas! There's something else! It's stunning. At the same time your blood produces the excess potassium your adrenal glands seem to enlarge on their own. They produce benign tumors like clockwork that seem to absorb this excess potassium for some reason! Do you know what this means?"

Nicolas broke out into tears. Not a hallucination. A memory. His dark and twisted memory.

"Shut up! Shut up, you sick-"

But the voice wouldn't go away.

"Nicolas, I think we should seriously perform some tests. Based on the data I have compiled it would appear that you have the basic static forecast for chronic Lazarus syndrome!"

"Playing God! They're playing God with me!" Nick couldn't control the tears. He couldn't remember much, but he'd remembered enough.

Enough to know that this didn't end until the tests failed.

* * *

The Mach 1 tore through the Durango countryside. Red dust bled through the air.

"Where else? Where would Nicky go if he was scared and couldn't head back to your old tree fort?" Marilyn's heart was hammering in her teeth.

"I-Hold on..."Alex leaned heavily against the back window. His eyes had light in them for the first time since Marilyn had gotten here. He had a purpose now. As much as it totally freaked him out, Nick was alive. He was his brother, for real this time. He was also apparently a murder victim for the second time this afternoon. If he had to move Heaven and Hell, Alex was going to save Nicky. He just had to figure out how.

"Watch it!" Renee screamed and covered her face with her hands.

He'd materialized center-street. It appeared the wild goose chase was over.

Marilyn brought the Mustang to a shrieking halt, drifting so hard to the left that they made a crescent moon of dust. It rolled over Nick like a tidal wave. He was painted scarlet as it stuck to his drenched clothes and hair.

Alex jumped out of the back seat. Felt his throat close. There he stood. Back from the dead. Scared out of his mind.

"Nick?" Alex called and raised his hands. It didn't matter. He felt like running to him and crunching his spine in his arms. He was alive. For the first time in a grief-stricken Eternity they were flesh and bone in the same air space.

"Nick, it's me, man. It's Alex." Alex took two stumbling steps forward. He couldn't contain himself. He ran to him.

Nick caught Alex as he flew like an inbound missile into his arms. He was sobbing into his shoulder without a care now. Even though he knew they couldn't stay here for long. There were people coming for Nick.

"Alex..."Nick gasped and pulled his brother closer.

"Yeah, it's me! Hey!" Alex was hysterical. He leaned up and grabbed Nick by both sides of his face. The boy swallowed and pressed his palms into Alex's chest.

"Dude, you're in danger."

"What?"

"They-these people- They're doing something to me. It's like a weird experiment. They kill me then they use some kind of mutated gene in my blood to bring me back to life again."

Nick was shaking without motor control. He kept twisting back in Alex's arms, trying to see behind him.

Alex forced Nick to turn around.

"Come with us."

There was the sound of approaching engines.

"Get in! Get in!" Renee was screaming at them from the car.

"Nick! How many times have we been over this?" One voice was shouting.

"Running is pointless. "The other belonged to a woman.

"Get in, boys!" Marilyn shrieked and drove forward. Renee did a backflip into the back seat. She kicked open the back door and held her arms out to haul them both in the moving car.

"Nicky, come with us. We can save you..." Alex's eyes were pleading.

"You won't be safe with me." Nick's lips twisted in nervous spasms.

"Nick, please. I can't live through your funeral again." Alex coughed, trying to keep his cool. Nick nodded. He was obviously terrified, but he knew he could trust his best friend.

They took to their heels. Renee grabbed Alex up from under his armpit. Alex grabbed Nick around the waist. The two boys and their caretaker all tumbled into the back seat. Renee hugged Nick and kissed his scalp, crying in overjoyed excitement. Alex leaned up and slammed the flapping door shut.

Marilyn watched the happy reunion in the rearview mirror with butterflies in her stomach. Now that she could see Nick for herself, she knew he belonged to her. From his expressions to his nose. He was her child, no questions.

She didn't get to enjoy laying eyes on her baby for the first time for very long. This happy reunion moment was shattered by the sound of gunfire.

"Whoa God!" Marilyn started to swerve serpentine style.

The valley Durango sits in is surrounded by huge conifers. Beautiful and treacherous for off-roading drivers.

"Hang onto your behinds, gang!" Marilyn put the car in neutral as they coasted off the road.

"Who are you?" Nick tried to sit up. Renee was hugging him from the front and Alex had his arms wrapped around him from behind making it almost impossible for him to move.

"Hello, Nicky. Here's another curve ball for you. My name is Marilyn Avalon. I am your birth mother."

CHAPTER 6

Nick's eyes crossed. He almost choked and looked into Renee's eyes incredulously.

"It's a long story. Just...don't ask. Don't say anything, Nicky." Renee held his face in her hands. She might not be his birth mother, but she loved him like he was her own child. He was back from the dead. For the second time. The world was spinning off its axis. That was okay. It could spiral away into the darkest part of the Universe for all she cared.

Dust swirled around them mixed with needles and branches. They could hear the loud baying of attack dogs. It was a blood-chilling sound, like the hounds of Hell, come to drag Lazarus back to whatever dark thing he'd left behind in the Afterlife.

A tree crashed onto its side in front of them. Marilyn popped the car back in drive having gained some ground and steered to the left. A razor blade of fire ran like electricity up the trunk. Smoke wafted in through the windows and they began to choke.

"Lady, listen to me! You have to give me back to them. They'll never give up until you do!" Nick was desperate leaping forward and leaning over Marilyn's shoulder.

"You're crazy! Over my dead body!" Marilyn's felt the blood of adrenaline laced desperation rush to her head.

"Actually, it's over my dead body. This-They're doing an experiment. It's something to do with potassium in my genes and some weird adrenaline thing. They're trying to figure out how to medically produce resurrection!" Nick beat his hand against the dash in agitation.

The car skidded in pine needles. There was a hiss. Their pursuers were lighting the woods on fire on purpose. Go figure.

"What?! That's insane!" Renee shook her head in horror.

"Maybe not! It's worked twice now, I guess. I can't really remember all that much." Nick's eyes were wild and his hair stood on end. Ashen around the lips, he looked back at Alex.

"They want Alex too. I don't know why. They just keep demanding I tell them where he is. He's in danger. You have to give me back."

"They want me for the experiment too, Nick. We have the same defect in our blood." Alex smiled sheepishly.

Nick laughed in surprise.

"Bummer. It's almost like we're related!"

"We are."

Nick tilted his head to the side.

"Nicky, we have the same birth father." Alex tried to clear his throat. The words felt heavy on his tongue. Every bit of this situation was surreal.

Nick slid to his knees in the floorboards. His mouth snapped open and closed like a baby bird trying to eat a worm.

"I'm your biological brother, Nick. Crazy, I know. But it's true." Alex smiled.

"What is this a family reunion?" Nick blinked wildly.

"It won't be if we all get killed." Marilyn looked over her shoulder. For the first time, she and her deceased/resurrected son were face to face. She swallowed. His green eyes were intense. Alive and in pain. Confused and hunted. She needed to save him. So that he could live to know his mother and that she did love him. Older and wiser now, she did love him and would only ever love him more.

"I need you to try and remember everything you can about these water-brains that are using you for Frankenstein drugs." Marilyn tried to level out her tone. She'd never been his mother before now and didn't really know where to even begin the whole "Mama" thing. She did, however, realize that if she wanted to level with this kid she couldn't tick him off from the get-go.

Nick licked his lips. Marilyn jerked the wheel. The trees were collapsing around them. Whoever they were, whatever their real motives, they would move Heaven and Nature to bag the monster they were creating.

"I don't know. It's...I...my head hurts. He's been taking my blood and x-rays and sticking needles in me. Told me I have, uh, chronic Lazarus syndrome. Whatever that means." Nick leaned against the passenger's seat eyes staring into Eternity.

"Oh God!" Marilyn looked back at Renee.

"What?" They all asked her at the same time.

"I know who it is. Or at least I know who one of them is."

"Who? Wait 'til I get my hands around their throat!" Renee's eyes popped in fury.

"You're not going to like it." Marilyn felt her head spinning. She should have seen this coming. How could she have not seen through the mask of perfect caring?

Renee swallowed.

"Wait...You think it's Dr. Swift?" Renee suddenly remembered their conversation on the porch. Dr. Swift had attributed Nicky's phenomenal resurrection to what he'd called Lazarus Syndrome. By the way he'd talked about it, he was obsessed with it. This and the fact that he'd been so confident and concerned about Alex's condition. He'd stressed relentlessly having him hospitalized for his psychological duress.

The devil was always in the details. How ironically frequent were these details on open display! They'd missed it because his concern had been so appropriate for his role. Because he'd just belonged there in the hour of need. He was the Doctor and so he fit.

Alex's eyes suddenly lit up.

"The Doc and my Dad. They had to have conspired together! He's the only one who would have known about both Nicky and me. He would have known about the gene too because he has to have been the one who passed it down to us. He's the only parent we share!" Alex hopped in his seat, hair standing on end.

"Ach! Yes, there are two of them. One's kind of a grunt. Taller. Older guy, older than the Doc he's like 40 something." Nick rubbed his forehead.

"Sounds like my dad." Alex swallowed and his hands shook.

"There's a woman too-"Nick didn't get the chance to finish this sentence. A silver Camaro came crashing through the trees. The driver bumped them.

The Mach 1 began to spiral in donut shapes. Their heads smashed the windows out and blood dripped into the cockpit. Through the dust, they could see her. The driver with beautiful golden hair.

Alex sat bolt upright, despite his injuries. He'd turned the gray/white color of sugar in his horror.

"Mom..."

CHAPTER 7

Alex bailed from the car, out of his head.

"Alex, wait!" Nick dove headfirst out of the back and caught him around the stomach.

"Mom!" Alex was hysterical. His dead loved ones were rising all around him with no plausible explanation other than his pediatrician and his father's psychotic experiments.

"Well, look who grew up handsome!" Mrs. Prescott swaggered into the dusty path. Her brows were raised and she was beaming. Marilyn got out of the car and stepped around it with extra caution.

"Oh, hello. You must be Army's whore. The one that gave life to this little bastard. Well, congratulations. It's marvelous, really. He's the best test subject we've ever had. Other than me, anyway." Mrs. Prescott grinned from ear to ear.

"You died of cancer. Like 5 years ago!" Renee's face blanched as she said this. She stepped out of the car and plucked a small pistol from a holster concealed on the inside of her bomber's jacket.

"Hey, now! Watch where you point that thing! I'm not overly keen on going back to the grave. Nicolas can relate." Mrs. Prescott flashed a menacing smile at Nick and blew him a kiss.

"Well, that depends. If I'm such a great test subject, then just take me and let these guys walk." Nick stepped forward. He shoved Alex behind himself with a graceful sweep of his arm.

"No way!" Alex grappled Nick's shoulder and thrust him back to standing side by side him. He threw a shielding arm in his way when he tried to step up again.

"Yeah, I think we've established that you have Lazarus Disorder, Nicky. That's what we're calling it anyway. The one disease that all of Humanity is quite literally dying to catch!" Mrs. Prescott fluffed her long golden hair and rolled her eyes. She was dancing in place, eager to give them the down low.

"Your dad, other than being the finest thing that ever walked the Earth, has that special something in his blood that can literally trigger the body to reanimate itself long before decomposing. Apparently, this lovely genetic defect can also reverse decomposition in human corpses! They submitted a gas form of his adrenal extract into my vault. After a period of three months, my body's decomposition had stopped. Further exposure to the gas plus electrical impulses being sent down my feet and hands and the decomposition was actually beginning to reverse. My body, while dead, was healing itself of decay. When I was a whole cadaver again, they began to inject me with the serum. They performed regular resuscitation attempts. I revived beautifully!" She laughed, a sadistic gleam in her eye.

"What a way to make up for having an affair! Army did feel really guilty about the three or four-night stands with you, Marilyn. I'm the one he really loved, you know. There's no real question of that now, is there? So, he raised me from the dead. Then he promised me that it would be your little bastard that we would make the guinea pig out of. While Alex would get the superfood from our harvest. We would inject him with those test results that worked. He'd be prime ready for the ROTC. To carry on in his father's footsteps as the ultimate soldier! Or basketball player! Or whatever he wanted to be! He would be the prime specimen of a human being on Earth. Whatever he became, he would be forever. Just let us have Alex. We're not going to hurt him. We'll make him immortal!" Whatever the psychotic experimentation had done, it had made her batty. She rolled her head on her neck, totally crazed.

"Look, I'm sorry about your many misfortunes in your previous life and this one. I had no idea that Army was married or I wouldn't have fooled around with him. What you've just said sounds like a lovely idea, but frankly it's straight up bull. That's the lie they've told you to get you to do what they want." Marilyn stepped forward and grabbed the boys by each of their shoulders.

"You're not touching either one of them ever again."

"You can't say that. Alex is mine."

"Yeah, no, not anymore. In the eyes of Colorado, Alex is hers." Marilyn pushed the boys behind Renee.

Mrs. Prescott laughed in their faces.

"That may be. Take him then. Good luck getting out of these woods."

Marilyn looked around. The forest was ablaze and the pace of the fire was only accelerating. Before they could think, they would be swallowed in it. Gone forever.

"If we can't have them, then nobody will. How do you cover your tracks? How do you wipe away blood stains in a world without enough tears to wet the mop? The answer is clean it all away with fire." Mrs. Prescott balled her hands in fists. Alex stared at his mother in horror. She was utterly changed by death, burial, and resurrection. However they had done it he didn't know. Whatever medical innovation they had attained that had brought her back had been a stroke of genius but totally unethical. By reviving her, they had altered her. Of all the sins that could be counted against them, this was the worst one.

Nick grabbed Alex suddenly and turned him to look in his eyes.

"I'm about to do something crazy. It's stupid and I could die again. But I don't care. My life is already over anyway, but yours has just begun. I want you to know that you're worth it." He clapped a hand on the side of Alex's face. His eyes were blazing. Alex shook his head in protest. Nicky Avalon couldn't be held down. Even the best efforts of Fate had failed to do this.

He ran forward and grappled Mrs. Prescott around the waist. He hauled her kicking and screaming to the roof of the Camaro.

"Army Prescott!" Nicky was shouting at the top of his lungs. It echoed off the trees. Everyone within a mile radius could hear his words.

"I'm calling you out, dude! I've got your wife. Now you've got to make a choice. I don't know what you're doing this for or why. You're going to end this, all of it, or else! If you don't come out and face me like a man, then I'll take steps. I will go to the press, the authorities, anybody! I'm taking her with me. You wanted the Fran kensteins walking the Earth. I'll give you Frankenstein and then some. Swallow that pill, if your gullet's big enough. I am Lazarus and I will take Durango by storm! Get ready, because here I go!"

With that he strong-armed Mrs. Prescott into the Camaro and took off into the blaze.

CHAPTER 8

This madness was thrust upon him and the ruins of his soul. Alex watched as his brother sped off to certain death. He was losing him all over again and there was nothing he could do about it. He was going to God-knew-what for his sake. It had been his choice.

Alex Prescott hadn't had much choice in his life. He'd always been the victim of circumstance. Yet today, as he watched his whole life going up in smoke around him, it woke up a fire within himself. He turned to face the women.

"It's too late. We can't get back in the car." He nodded, indicatively. Marilyn's jaw dropped. The Mach 1 was ablaze.

"We don't have much time. You guys had better listen to me carefully." Alex swallowed, knowing what kind of reaction this was going to trigger.

"What? No, listen, Alex. You're- I'm legally responsible for you!" Renee jabbed a finger at him.

"I'm a professional!" Marilyn began. Alex held up a hand.

"Save it, both of you. This isn't your battle and you can obviously see it. They want me. I'm the hot potato in this Game and you know it. I'm pretty good at playing keep-away. I've been bounced around the world my entire life. That's exactly what I'm going to do. It's my responsibility. That's my mom and brother out there, got it? I don't really care what happens to me-"

"Alex, listen, buddy, nobody else is going to die..." Renee's voice was quivering. She could barely contain the tears.

"Heck no! It's definitely not going to be him. I swear to God, I will never bury my brother again. You'll have to break my legs to stop me. This is my choice. My responsibility. The rest is up to you guys. I'll play this Game for as long as I can. But there's only so far you can run when you're running in circles. It's all teamwork from here on out. You've got to pull this off. Get to the bottom of their motives. Bust this up before Durango goes down in flames." Alex nodded. It was done. He might die, but, at least, he'd die having made a choice of his own for once. He shook his head.

"I'll haunt you for the rest of Eternity if you don't." He laughed, with a tiny shrug.

Renee nodded, unable to keep herself from crying.

"Okay. I promise, Alex. It's...It's going to be okay."

He nodded.

"See ya around..."

"Wait!" Renee gasped and stepped forward.

"You'll need this more than I will, I think. Your mom seemed kind of off her roller coaster when she said all that she did." She pressed the gun into Alex's hand.

He smiled one last calm smile.

"Take care of my New Mom, Marilyn." It was a command. Marilyn felt her stomach burn like she'd swallowed a fistful of batteries.

"You got it, man."

He took two steps off into the blaze, jaw squared.

"Yo! Morons! You want a test gerbil? Come and get me!" He aimed the gun at the air and nothing and fired off a round to draw their attention. Other voices shouted from the shadows of the blaze. Dogs howled. Suddenly terrified, seeing something they couldn't, Alex bolted into the collapsing forest.

In the confusion and anguish, Marilyn had almost forgotten her blazing car.

"Get down!" She leaped and knocked Renee onto her face. There was a moment of silence as if maybe her fears were unfounded. Then it happened and the sound was so loud they felt it more than they heard it. Dust, frost capped mosses, tree roots and stones covered them. They lay in the dark of the debris. Their ears were ringing and that was the only intelligible sound they heard as they faded away into unconsciousness.

CHAPTER 9

Waking up in a blazing forest is not for the faint of heart.

Marilyn got up on her elbows. She looked down to notice that Renee was lying beside her, choking on the cinders of half-burned leaves.

"Come on. I know what to do. Believe it or not, I've done this before."

Marilyn reached and took a few fistfuls of ashes. She rubbed it in their hair and on their faces. Then she tore out of her coat and ran it through the ashes. She swept it over both their heads and made a run for it.

The forest was black with smoke. Something else was obviously on fire in it. Not just the Mustang. Marilyn's beloved Mach 1 had given up the ghost around 45 minutes ago, which was probably the same time they'd tapped out.

They charged through the forest afraid of the worst. The silver Camaro was abandoned in a ravine, turned over on its head.

"No!" Renee stumbled to her knees and fell just as a series of mostly flame-consumed tree branches floated through the air where she'd been standing.

"It's been flipped on purpose. It was hardly even damaged before it started burning, see? There're blazing boots and a jacket stuffed with a barbecued pair of hands. Looks like Nicky's decided to get really inventive to shake these clowns." Marilyn ran to the Camaro. There would have to be an explanation for where her son had gotten the fake limbs to produce such a make-shift prop in the middle of his mad-dash escape.

The trunk was pushed down but not locked. Inside was a disturbing assortment of freezer bags that contained-

"Ah God!" Marilyn gasped. She recognized them at once.

"Human remains! See the numbers on the sides of the bags. These are specific labels. These jokers ripped off a local mortuary to get this stuff. The wife was transporting it. Which should tell you something."

Renee's eyes were bugging and she was green around the mouth.

"Ehem, okay. Should it be telling me that these people are sadistic freaks that need to burn in hell?" She cringed and clenched her fist.

"Well, that too. I was going to say that clearly the adrenal extra must have been so effective they want to move on to a wider variety of testing. Remember how Prescott's wife was saying something about how they cured her corpse of decomposition before they tried to resuscitate her? These pieces of people..." Marilyn didn't feel like the rest needed to be explained.

"That's wrong on a number of levels." Renee covered her mouth, fighting the urge to vomit.

"Yes. This is also how Nick got a convincing set of hands and feet and a few femurs to fill his fake-death dummy with. See, the only part of the car that's burning are the tires. The body's in the interior which thanks to all this dirt is flame free for now. So why is it burned? It could only mean that the victim he filled his jacket and boots with must have died by burning and so he just improvised. See, the car isn't damaged, aside from the paint job damage where it flipped on its head." Marilyn leaned through the ajar driver's side window to confirm her suspicion.

He parked it on the tip of this hill rise here and threw it into neutral..." Marilyn was more of a rescue worker than she was a detective. She knew how to look for signs of a person's presence, even if they'd been missing for decades. On a roll now, she climbed the hill again.

"See, his bare footprint. He removed the necessary clothes, used the elements to damage them for stage effect and dressed up the dummy. Then he pushed the car and had Mrs. Prescott help him. That's a woman's shoe. See the way it's shaped? These are fresh too. They couldn't be older than an hour. Which means it happened shortly after he pulled his debonair escape. He must have assumed that the flames would eventually further damage the car. Which would lead Dr. Swift and Prescott

to assume he'd been consumed in the blazes." Marilyn's eyes twinkled. Her son was scary clever.

"With what the wife said about cleaning up with fire, they must not know how to heal a cadaver of fire damage yet. Which would explain why the body parts were all from burning victims. That's what they need to research." Renee laughed. This strategy was actually amazing.

"With Nick and Mrs. Prescott assumed dead all the focus will now train to Alex. Which is what Nicky wants. The closer Alex is to danger, the more they assume that Nick is no longer in the picture, the better he can protect him because they won't see him coming to the rescue!" Marilyn was dancing in place with excitement now.

"Alex is the master of keep away. Whatever Nicky's going to do to one-up these guys, he can take all the time he needs!" Renee looked back at the crash, beaming.

"I have drawn a startling inspiration from these remains, Ms. Vierra." Marilyn eyed the contents of the trunk again as some nasty little plan was forming in the back of her mind.

'You've lost me?" Renee's eyebrows curled in unison.

"Sometimes to do a good deed, you've got to pretend to be the villain. I've got an old spark with Army Prescott that could use some fanning into flame. Don't try and understand. Consider me the Queen of Diamonds in this neck-breaking run for the money. You can be the Queen of Hearts and do your home mother thing, girl. The boys are going to need you doing what you do best."

Marilyn pulled out her phone. She had Army's number. Not his old one, but his new one. She'd gotten it from his sister. It had been a few months ago, but in a weak moment she'd thought about giving him a ring.

Now she knew exactly what to do. She smiled to herself. This was cold.

Not as cold as turning your child into Frankenstein. A woman scorned is one thing to beware. But a mother scorned is a holy terror even the Devil would be reluctant to bait.

CHAPTER 10

Alex was walking past the new favorite bar in Durango, a hood pulled over his face. The light from the TVs shone in his emerald eyes. He ducked his head and shoved his hands into his pockets. He needed to press into the chatter. To make certain for himself that Nicky and his mother had made it out of the forest.

He'd barely gotten away with his life. What he had seen was enough to send him to an early grave. It was too much. These were actions that the Heavens could never forgive.

People were pushing to be closer to the TVs in the bar. One could watch them from the sidewalk, which is what most of the gathered had resorted to doing as the bar was now swamped.

The screens were playing back scene after scene of Nick's bizarre recovery in Lake Nighthorse. The screen flashed from the playback footage to Chief Riggs who was being interviewed. Apparently to his great irritation.

"Yes, we were made aware that Nicolas Avalon had up and stepped out of the box. However, as trained professionals and protectors of this amiable City we had elected as an official body not to alert the public to avoid exactly what is happening now. Sheer panic. The fact that the boy has appeared on his own and has allegedly resurrected for the second time is still a mystery to the police force. We have had some anonymous tipsters come forward blaming the whole thing on a local Dr. Death that is inexplicably MIA at the moment." Chief Riggs' speech was stilted and rehearsed. Alex smiled to himself. He knew this meant that Marilyn and Renee had come up with a plan and had tipped the Chief off to it.

"Yes, it's working out beautifully, don't you think?" A familiar voice spoke beside him.

Alex turned to face the woman that had just elbowed her way to the window. It was Renee, her identity mostly concealed by a brown Stetson.

"You made it!" Alex could have hugged her.

"You too, buddy. Impressive." She winked and coughed into her fist.

"Hey, that's my friend in there. She has a son about your age. If you live here for a long time, maybe the two of you could hang out." Renee started talking in a sort of double-speak to tip Alex off without alerting anyone else. He followed her eyes to where Marilyn sat on a bar stool, holding a cocktail and drilling her high-heeled shoe into the linoleum floor.

Alex turned to Renee brows curled in confusion.

"She's had a hard time since her son was born, you know? He had a fraternal twin sister that was stillborn. I guess she went in there to meet up with the dad and talk it out. She was too ashamed and felt like it was her fault that one of the babies didn't make it. She thinks that the dad needs to know the whole truth, or else its bad karma." Renee rubbed the back of her neck, hoping her double-speech was convincing enough.

Both of them had two much information to exchange here. Alex smiled and nodded, thinking out his own double-speak.

"I'm sorry to hear that. Yeah, I've seen my share of death and terrible things too. I was in the woods once and I witnessed a heinous crime. It really jarred my faith in Humanity." He didn't finish what he was saying. The broadcast was interrupted suddenly by a live video feed being shot in the back of a news truck.

Nicky leaned close to the camera, smiling darkly in the lights of all the digital machinery.

"Hello, adoring public of Durango. My name is Nicolas Avalon. Yes, I died 7 months ago in a vehicular homicide and also a few hours ago in the bottom of Lake Nighthorse. Yes, obviously, I am alive again. I am the victim not of murder but of a sadistic scientific research program that is being headed up in your very own community.

Not to worry. I'm certain Chief Riggs will be able to secure the city and your civilian safety will be taken into total consideration when dealing with this threat. I interrupt your newscast to send a private message to one of the players in this Death Game.

Dr. Lucien Swift. I have been informed by a very reliable source-" Nicky leaned his head back to indicate where Prescott's wife sat handcuffed to him in the opposite chair.

"Where your other victims are. Some of them are not in their best wits and would be more than happy to help me cause you limitless pain. I have acquired the means from my trusty snitch to liberate these oppressed dead people from your confinement. You and all of Durango will suffer the rising of the Witnesses if you fail to turn yourself in within the next 48 hours."

The feed cut off. The camera went black for a moment and then switched back to a view of Chief Riggs standing with the evening news reporter Erin Pickler.

"Oh my God, it's happening." Alex covered his mouth in a shaking hand. Renee stared at him, dying to pick his brain.

CHAPTER 11

Marilyn stared in horror and almost knocked over the Tom Collin's she had in front of her. This situation was only continually spiraling into a darker, more confused place. Here in Durango Humanity had failed. Now the whole City could see it and soon so would the rest of the United States. After the States then the World.

"He's got your charms." His voice startled her and took her home to younger days all in the same breath. Marilyn spun around on her stool. There stood Army Prescott, older now, but still just as handsome as he'd been. He was wearing the jacket from his uniform. This made her heart twist.

"Army..." She choked on his name as he sat down.

"Rusty Nail for me thanks." Army winked at the bartender and sat down, leaning over his hands to look into Marilyn's face.

"It's been too long..." His voice was satin. She swallowed the sting of the years. He smiled as the drink was set in front of him, threw a handful of bills on the counter and turned back to her with tender eyes and drawing a long drink.

Drifting to them from somewhere behind the counter, the sad riffs of the Eagles "Desperado" began to play. Marilyn swallowed and watched as Army pulled a Hemingway from his shirt pocket and cut the cap with a lady's nail file. She felt her throat get tight as she gaped at the bad boy in front of her remembering why he was so attractive to her in long gone days. He plucked a match out of his wallet and lit it against the brickwork of the counter, lighting the cigar's foot as his eyes twinkled in the flame.

"You called me pretty broken up. Yeah, I know this stuff with Nicky is seriously warped. Trust me, it wasn't my idea. I was trying to save him."

Of course, she didn't believe him. No man allows his child to be turned into

Frankenstein's monster because he was "trying to save him". It was sick and against the laws of nature. She felt rage foaming like rabies in the pit of her stomach.

"Don't lie to me, you sultry SOB. I read you like tabloids and what I see is just as cheap. You did it because you profited from it somehow. You've always been interested in speed, Prescott. Fast women, fast cash, fast cars, and no consequences. Oh, you're a beautiful sinner, there's no question of that. How much did you sell our son for, huh? How many thousands?" She smiled as her eyebrow curled. His nose twitched.

"Don't talk down to me, Avalon. You didn't exactly come here to pass out Bibles, did you? Fine, so I had my own kid iced for medical research. It's not like I'd been to his soccer games or anything. How does it make it any better just because his sister died right after she was born, huh? You're still selling her body for research. That's really no better than medical prostitution if you want my opinion."

Marilyn clenched her teeth. She just had to pretend this was Texas Hold 'Em. With one massive swallow, she plucked a shoe box from her coat.

"So, I'm no saint either. I lied. I've cheated and I steal. I've done something far worse this time. It was so bad I couldn't keep the other baby. So bad that I couldn't tell you, even though I felt like telling you about your son would make you want to come back." Marilyn tilted her head to the side. Of course, this was all a bluff. There had never been another baby. This was her play. The wicked plan she'd made in the midst of the forest fire. She'd used parts from the Camaro wreck and Renee's critique to make it convincing too.

"She was stillborn. They usually give you the baby to bury or whatever. Well, I pretended to bury her, but it was really one of those freakishly creepy life-like dolls in the coffin. This box contains her real body. I had her taxidermied. There was a man, a really good taxidermist who wanted to try it on a human. It worked horribly as human skin just isn't made for stuffing...I kept her even like this at the foot of my bed. In this box all this time. It was the sick fetish of a confused, alcoholic woman! Apparently the Devil wouldn't leave it alone. Now here she is. Preserved with some embalming techniques that have kept her spinal fluid, her hair, and everything. The thing is though the reason she was still born is the doctor's be-lieved there were some very peculiar anomalies with the development of her heart and adrenal glands. She had renal failure in utero and hyperkalemia as a result of this. Your guess is as good as mine, Cassanova. But you can take her. I don't want a dead baby if I could have a living son! Take the baby and give Nicky back to me! Go back to your sick science kitchen and leave my boy alone!"

Her performance should have won her an Oscar. He'd bought it. Hook, line and sinker. She could tell by the green that stretched up his cheek and splashed across his temples.

Laughter coursed through him and he slapped his knee down, spilling the Rusty Nail all over the counter. Matty the bartender spun on her boot heel, irritated. She swatted a rag and began to clean it up.

That moment he'd slapped his knee was all it had taken. Marilyn gingerly slipped the cuffs out of her pocket and clicked one end of them around his wrist. She clicked the other around hers while he was wheeze laughing to tears and couldn't even hear it.

"Oh, darling! You think I'd actually buy that bill of goods? Even if you're telling the truth, which you're totally not because you, darling, totally suck at the Poker face... Why would I accept a butchered dead baby over a living, strapping, healthy teen-aged guinea pig boy?"

"Ah, well, see about that. I didn't need you to buy it. I just needed to sell it. Which is exactly what I just did. Got your whole voice-over right hear. Pretty as a Nashville record. Let me say it for the tape, though. The contents of this box are not human remains. This is the small fetus of a chimpanzee that was donated to the medical center for pathologist interns to practice on. It was found in the Camaro wreck 6 miles from Lake Nighthorse on the western half of the Lake and should be filed under evidence from the wreck if anything has survived the fire."

Marilyn punched a button on her cell phone. Army could clearly see from the screen that his confession had just been recorded. Of course, leave it to a private investigator to pull some kind of stint such as this.

"Now, ahem, you remember that little favor you promised to do for 20 bucks?" Marilyn turned to Matty laughing and slapped a bill on the table.

Matty swung herself up on top of the counter. She plucked a 45 cal from where it leaned against her side of the fence and loaded it with graceful fingers and a wink at Army.

"That was just a joke, lady. Hang around Durango for a little while longer and you'll see. This is the West, darlin'. We do these kinds of favors for free!" Matty affected her accent a little to tease Marilyn. She hopped down from the counter and trained the rifle's barrel to the back of Army's head.

"You might not have known this, mister, but I'm the bartender, bouncer and dishwasher all rolled into one. It's time for you to beat it." She whistled through her teeth with a hard laugh.

They lead Army outside the both of them singing "Rawhide" just to annoy him. Renee sat in her Datsun listening to an old 3 Doors Down CD that Alex had left in the player.

"Wassup! Bagged that rattler did ya? Alright! Let's take him downtown. Besides, Alex tipped me off anyway. There's something you got to see!" Renee's eyes were blazing as she turned over the key. Marilyn forced Army into the back and chained him to another chain that was woven up through a hole in the trunk and was wrapped around 6 concrete blocks that were inside the trunk.

"Yeah, we thought about you trying to slip your chains. We took steps where it won't happen. Now, stick a sock in it." Marilyn shoved a knot made of Alex's discarded socks into Army's teeth. Renee cranked the radio and they shot off into the gathering dark.

CHAPTER 12

Alex stood in the woods, dancing to shift the cold in his feet. He'd used his GPS and Mathlete computation skills to figure out his exact coordinates. Marilyn, Renee, and his captive dad should be here any minute, the police in their wake.

It had been a simple realization of the Wandering Hot Potato. Despite their masks and military coats, he had a maturing boy's eyes. He could spot the female figure from a mile away. Thus, Alex Prescott had concluded that the entire nursing staff of Durango general hospital were accomplices to Dr. Lucien Swift's crime. Playing on his conclusions, he had sent a blanket text to everyone on Lucien's contact list (which he had stolen by hacking into his email).

All he could do now was watch and wait. Wait to be caught between the scalpels of crazed physicians and the teeth and inhumanly strong hands of the angry risen dead.

From where he stood, Alex smelled fire. He could see the tongues off it licking up from the center of a stump that Nicky was standing on.

Nick stood with his arms spread in the Crucifix position. His eyes were gleaming in the glow of the embers that burned around his ankles. From where he stood, Alex could feel the rage that echoed into the deepest circle of his brother's tormented soul. To have been called back from his blood-drenched grave only to become the most sought after lab-rat of the Century was beyond demeaning. Knowing now that he was not the only one was empowering. He stood to incite rage in those dredged from the dust.

Alex held his breath. This had been the terrible thing he had seen and had tipped Renee off to at the bar. The forests surrounding Lake Nighthorse had become a garden of harvested corpses. Dracula could have done no better. They hung from trees, some only partially reversed from their natural decomposing and still by def-inition dead. Then some of them hung healed of decomposing and were reviving slowly from the extract. Then there were those who hung from the trees gasping for reanimated breath. They were writhing incessantly mid-air, trying to free themselves of the nylon ropes that suspended them from branches in "X" shapes.

These that were awake had their eyes wide open and their heads fully turned to Nick where he stood in the midst of the smoke.

He picked up a piece of cardboard he'd leaned against the trunk and had written on with a permanent marker. The Hanging People twisted around to read his sign:

This is the Forest of Toys for the God-players. Abandon hope all that enter here.

"Ladies and gentlemen!" Nick's voice echoed off the trees and drowned out the whimpering of a once-teenaged girl that had just revived.

"Can everyone hear me? Are you awake yet? Feel like you've been asleep for centuries? For some of you, this is actually true."

A man that was hanging in the rotten clothes of a historical cowboy choked audibly, astounded by Nick's implication.

"Listen to me all of you. My name is Nicolas Avalon. Over half a year ago I was killed in a traffic accident. I was murdered by people my own father had solicited for the sake of medical research! Then by some divinely successful stroke of that same research I revived. Again I was drowned in the Lake, not 10 miles from here. Again, I was revived.

I have come forward to campaign for you, ladies and gentlemen, citizens of the Grave. I don't know how long this scientific phenomenon will sustain us. Could it be that it is temporary and we will return to the casket linens shortly? I have no idea. Or shall we live our lives again to full ripe age? I don't have an answer for this either. Is this a blessing or a curse? It's beyond me."

He swallowed, knowing what he was saying was a difficult sermon to hear. But he needed to say it. For the sake of his own free moral agency, he needed to preach his conviction to these people.

"What I do know for absolutely certain, ladies and gentlemen, is that a great wrong has been done to us all. We are just warm-blooded dolls with respiration in the games of these God-players. What we are isn't natural. Didn't we have the right to rest in peace? Is it morally right or actually ethical to disturb our Eternal rest and submit us to these excruciating examinations? My good citizens of the Grave, the answer is no! This thing that has been done to us is intolerable!"

There were murmurs of almost unanimous agreement among those who were awake. One small boy was curiously eyeing one of the hanging cadavers as his own lips turned a bright lime green. The others saw his horror and the atrocity was driven home. It was the farthest thing from natural. It was unacceptable.

"All I feel is pain, from the top of my head to the tips of my toes. Pain and excessive hunger! It's like I have billions of tiny nails being driven into me with little chisels. Chipping me away, filling me with an emptiness that can't be appeased. A disease that can't be cured! My heart beat is agonizing. With every beat, I feel like I am being sprayed with bullets! You feel it too! I have no doubt!" Nick tore at his clothes. He was unable to control the quivering in his voice.

"I am not going to just lay down and let them kill me and then zap me back awake! Over and over again. Like I was some kind of frog to be dissected! I don't know what the rest of you are going to do. But I'm going to stand up to these God-players! I'm going to fight back. If I have to live against the natural grain of my life that's already over, then they will too! There will be fire. We will roast this place off the map. You could see it from Jupiter!"

Now there was a shout from the Waking Ones. Their cry was one battle anthem. A provoked fury rising from the mortal ice. The Dead had been displaced. They would not be quick to forgive.

Alex held his breath. Behind him, he heard the engines of the police squad cars coming to the Calvary. He heard the rumbling of mobile Lab truck engines.

It was all falling into place now. News cameras and vlogger sensations tuning into every corner of the Internet. The world was ready to see the great battle for the sanctity of Human will. The corruption of Human life. The deciding battle of the 'Science of Resurrection.'

CHAPTER 13

"Prisoner's in the car. His statement's on tape." Marilyn hopped out of the Datsun's shotgun seat and tossed Chief Riggs her phone.

"I don't hand out the props over easy, Avalon. Gotta say it now. Good job." The Chief tipped his hat to her.

Renee hopped out of the driver's seat and looked into the misty evening forest. Her eyes popped when she saw the smoke and Nicky standing in the center of the fire.

"I told you. This has gone beyond the realm of what is and what never should be..." Alex was invisible in the shadow of the trees. His voice trembled with rage beyond relent.

"Taking it you've found out more than you let on over the phone, kid." Chief Riggs stepped deeper into the shadows and drew back astonished. Something wasn't right with Alex.

"Some things you have to do in person. In private preferably, but that's not really an option this time. I saw something in the forest. It might be the end of me. But I had to. I was the one they wanted to do tests on next...My brother has suffered enough."

Alex stepped out of the shadows. Renee covered her mouth.

Having plucked his coat off, they could now see that the boy was wearing a body armor vest that was affixed with 6 additional hearts each matched with 6 adrenal glands.

"I'm sorry to have to be the one to solve the mystery. Really, I am. It's not the story I'd like to tell. Yes, I'm pretty good at Hot Potato. You know the saying that words have power? Words took me down like a fighter jet. I had to make a choice. It was either add one more heart to this vest or wear it myself. See, I love my brother. You have no idea what it's like unless you've got one of your own. I couldn't let him die again. Sorry...I don't know how to explain...Let me explain." Alex coughed and held up his hand. His eyes were squinted almost entirely closed pained by even the dim light.

Renee felt herself break into tears. She was amazed that he could have hidden his agony so well when they were standing outside of the bar.

"My dad was pretty high up the totem pole of military rank before he was honorably discharged for critical wounds he got in an Afghani firefight. When he came home, Mom always said he was obsessed with medical research. It wasn't just his own recovery that interested him either. When he was in the hospital, he found himself totally wrapped up in a project that meant to study battlefield resuscitation processes and rapid wound closing. My dad submitted his own blood samples to the supposedly good cause.

They say that bad company ruins good morals. Looks like whoever coined that one got it right, huh? Lucien Swift was a pediatric surgeon that worked under the same research hospital umbrella my father was treated by. That's how they met each other. It was Lucien's gung-ho involvement in the study and research of my Dad's "evolutionary adrenal anomalies" that finally influenced him to become the guinea pig for the test himself. The United States government funded the research program with the intention that it would eventually produce them with "self-resuscitating hybrid soldiers". GI prodigies that had the ability to adapt the size of their adrenal glands and to make extra of muscle function helping chemicals-like potassium- to actually resuscitate themselves naturally. A harnessed version of what's called Lazarus syndrome. Like Darwinism meets Zombie Sparta or something, I don't know.

Certain members of our government abused their power and used personal funding from the culprits' individual bank books, and founded Santa Bianca's Children's Home here in Durango about 22 years ago. It was meant to be a satellite foster home they could dump all the offspring of Test Subject# 1(my Dad) off to and harvest for the research work. See, every kid that lives or has lived in Santa Bianca's is actually my dad's biological kid. As part of the program, my dad had to donate sperm for loads of women to be artificially inseminated with so there could be as many potential subjects as possible. He was also under strict orders to experiment with different substances and to have sex with as many women as he could seduce, assuming that eventually babies would come out of all of it. They needed to see if any of the factors of biochemical substances or the process of physical intimacy would alter the test subjects."

Alex looked down at his chest. Now he was shaking, about to be sick.

"It turns out that my Dad has so far had exactly 8 kids that were a result of these ordered love affairs. I'm one of them. Nicky is another. These guys' organs here were our 6 brothers..."

Alex looked to the sky tears forming in his eyes. He grit his teeth as the vest obviously caused him extreme pain.

"A corrupted team of Black Ops officials were under orders. The test subjects themselves were to be strategically assassinated under varying circumstances to see how resuscitation would work under every kind of death. My brothers here were killed in a car wreck about 4 years ago. They tried and failed to cause the Lazarus syndrome in them. That's why their organs were deposited for the study of using another subject's organs to regulate this stimulated resuscitation or whatever.

Then the women that were intimate with my dad were targeted. They were trying to see if the process of chemical reaction in the brain when people get together like that could make the subjects' react to what's now known as the "Prescott1" adrenal extract. They wanted to do this with women he'd only been with once or a few times, like Detective Avalon, and someone he'd been with for years like my Mom. She was exposed to a large amount of those cancer chemical things when my parents were married to influence the process of cancer they were actually inducing in her. I don't know how they do it, but then they can do a lot of crap apparently! Anyway, they killed my mom so they could try and bring her back to life. They lured Detective Avalon to Durango so they could attempt to whack her and use her for the project too."

Alex clawed at himself and looked down.

"All the tests were almost ready for moving on to marketing. All they needed to do was see if they could use radiation and chemical exposure in decomposed test subjects and bring them back. That would include some of my Dad's ancestors. Dad is from Colorado. His whole family is from the Durango area. That's why the study was done here. So that when we reached this chapter...They'd have my dead relatives to dig up and have a little fun with..."

The effort to muster the breath for this explanatory monolog had caused Alex intense pain. He bowed himself and coughed up blood. Then he clutched at his throat and make a sound like a dying bull-frog.

"The vest...Why are you?" Renee was on the verge of mental breakdown.

"This thing is kinda like a life support device or something. It pumps my body's blood 6 times as fast because it works these 6 hearts on a battery to do it. It uses these 6 adrenal glands to enhance my performance. S'posed to anyway... It's better to use real hearts than a machine, eh? That's what they told me. All I know is it's killing me to wear and if I take it off...I'mma have a heart attack!" His voice was dying away now and his lips were turning purple. He clutched at his knees crying from the effort it had taken to speak.

There was sudden applause.

"Wonderful explanation, Alexander! You might have been a great man someday."

All eyes fell on Dr. Swift as he emerged from the smoke. Every officer present pulled his weapon.

"You know, the good soldier's like you, Alex, weren't meant to be casualties of this experiment. I never wanted violence and I wouldn't call it murder either. I had all faith that my science could heal all of you. Don't you see? We had conquered

Death! Before him anyway..."

Swift's face had so drastically changed from the kind doctor Marilyn had met such a short time ago at Santa Bianca's. Now it was livid green and twisted by the mania raving inside of him.

"The Program did have a certain protocol in place. We had to prepare for the eventuality of a rebel like Nicolas. A self-resurrecting soldier that cannot be controlled is like a nuclear weapon that can be used by anyone. So we took additional steps to ensure that there was an eventual death for immortal Lazarus." Lucien produced a syringe with a clear liquid.

"I still believe firmly in my science. Like the Grecians of old, I will have to face the critics and the firing squads for my radical achievements. I am not, however, an evil person. I have cured the World of Death. At the same time, I have abolished the likelihood of legal encroachment. There will be no more rebels. No more dying. No fear or pain! I gave you fools Utopia! I and my mad science and my raving disciples. I will walk willingly to whatever end you and the uncorrupted Federal body allows for me. There is no greater ambition in my mind than to be the last martyr of science. The greats that come after me will, of course, be cured of the possibility. I have one last work to accomplish. I must rid the Earth of Nicolas Avalon!"

It happened instantaneously. There was no time to logically map out the next steps. Marilyn leaped forward and caught Renee and Alex under her arms. She dropped to the ground and covered their heads.

Lucien had thrown down a small canister of tear gas. The officers reeled. Then there was a sound of insurgence as the Dead broke free. Nick's voice could be heard shouting something rousting over the din of angry rabble.

This didn't end well for anyone.

CHAPTER 14

Marilyn felt her throat closing under the drug's effects. There was a trampling commotion out in the midst of the woods. Alex was gagging and making sounds that belonged in a horror flick. Marilyn twisted around in the midst to see him in the throes of a severe seizure on the ground beside her.

"I've got him! You go after your boy!" Renee choked out the words and waved Marilyn on.

It was madness. She felt so small in the midst of it. People ran in figure eights. Officers were trying to infiltrate the scene. SWAT teams filed into the fumes, faces hidden under reflector shields of plexiglass. If Marilyn had ever wondered she now knew what a battlefield in the Civil War would have been like.

"It doesn't work on us, Doctor! You did your job too well!" Nick's voice. So confident and uncaring faced with his third death this year.

The Wakers hadn't actually armed themselves. They were equipped only with their fury. This might be enough. Research assistants screamed from the forest. The Dead had come for them and they could not get away.

Marilyn broke through the trees. She stopped dead in her tracks.

It was sheer frenzy. They moved in circles like a helicopter's blades. Nick's torment had turned him into something almost animal. Voraciously savage. He jabbed his fist into Lucien's throat with the direct lunging action of a cobra bite, letting his fingernails tear into his skin. The Doctor coughed and bowed over his knees. Nick kicked him until he collapsed.

He stood looming over him with an almost wicked smile spread across his features.

"Some God you are now, huh." Nick hesitated, tilting his head to the side.

"I could kill you. I honestly should kill you. Somehow taking your life is almost as bad as you waking me up from the Dirt Nap. As much as it physically sickens me to actually do this, I think I'm going to let you live, Doctor." Nick had to literally overpower himself, swinging his shoulders and pivoting his skyscraping frame to back away. Marilyn held her breath. The baby she had given away had become a mature adult.

Mercy had been Nick's mistake. Dr. Swift was motivated by a scientific obsession that outweighed his physical needs. With a shriek that shook the valley, he dove forward and grabbed Nick's legs. He dug in his fingers climbing him like a cat will drapes. Thrusting forward, he pierced the syringe into his heart.

Nick froze. His eyes went wide.

Marilyn dug her heels into the ground. Knowing he'd died before was one thing. Seeing him die was wholly something else.

His lips began to foam and tears were wrenched from his eyes.

"I've...I've cured you. See, that makes us even!" Lucien had his tongue stuck out sickly and was chuckling through his teeth.

There was a sudden gunshot that rang out across the trees.

"Some things you've got to take care of yourself." Chief Riggs declared as he stood with the Sig Sauer smoking in his hand.

Lucien groaned and fell forward. The Chief had shot him in the back and the bullet had gone all the way to his heart.

"Nick!"

Marilyn dove forward like an All-Star baseball player coming for the Home run.

Nick gurgled on his over-salivation and collapsed backward. He lay staring at the sky in a drugged haze, clueless to his dying all over again.

"Nick! No! No, it's okay. It's okay. I've got you!"

Marilyn collapsed next to him and scooped him up. For the first time in his life, she cradled her child in her arms.

"No, Nick. Not again, buddy...I've...I've got so much to tell you! Look at me!" Nick's head began to roll toward the ground. Marilyn lifted his face, forced him to look up into her eyes.

"I'm your Mom, Nicky. You've got to live, buddy. So that we can know each other and be family!"

She was crying all of the sudden. For the life that she'd missed out on. For the things that had been done to her son. Maybe if she'd kept him none of it would have happened? She told herself that there was nothing she could have done, but it didn't help with the pain of this moment. Of watching the light fading in his evergreen eyes.

"Mom?" He asked, smiling. He'd never gotten to say that before.

"Hang on, buddy. I'm going to get you some help."

CHAPTER 15

"By God, Alex! I"m done burying kids! You're going to make it, son. Come on!"

Renee pulled Alex up over her shoulder. He was thrashing, eyes rolling in his head like a crazy horse. He looked at her desperately confused. For most of us, death approaches like a fever slow and serene. For Alex, it had come with the force of the ocean savage in power. He was drowning in his own blood as his nostril vessels began to rupture and the roof of his mouth split with the seven times stronger rush of his blood on the six amplified hearts plus his natural one.

Renee drug Alex thrashing to where the Datsun still loomed like an island amidst the tear gas.

"What the hell is going on?! What's wrong with him?!" Army shouted as Renee jerked the door open.

She swung her fist across his face so hard he flew into the back window and cracked the glass.

"You've lost the right to even ask that question when you put him in the line of fire!" Renee shouted above the din of voices. She swiped and grappled the front of his jacket. Hauling him upward as far as his chains would go, she forced him to look her in the tear-gas inflamed eyes. Army had faced whole battalions of Taliban fighters in his day and had never broken a sweat. He was trembling in front of her.

"Just this once, you are going to be a good father to one of your many sons and hold him still. Press my belt between his teeth so he doesn't bite off his tongue!" Renee ripped her belt off and twisted around to Alex.

"Hey, buddy, look up here. Hi..." She smiled at him and pushed his sweat-drenched hair off his forehead.

"Promise this won't hurt." She reached and pried his mouth open pushing the belt between his teeth not a minute too soon. He clamped his teeth down hard enough that the enamel cracking was audible.

"Easy now, kiddo. Your dad's here in the back. I'm going to pass you off to him, okay?" Renee carefully started to drag Alex toward the backseat. He thrashed, terrified at the thought of being face to face with his psycho-studies Dad.

"Seriously, it'll be okay. I'm not going to let him do any more mad science on you. He tries and I'll kill him." Renee finally laid Alex down. She snapped around in surprise just as she'd laid Alex's twisting body directly in Army's lap.

"You'd kill my husband?!" It was Mrs. Prescott. She'd finally escaped Nick's custody. She'd soared in mind-altered devotion to the rescue of the man that had subjected her to her sadistic and ridiculous existence.

"If he tries to do any further damage to your son? Yeah." Renee brought her fists up in a boxer's stance.

Mrs. Prescott pulled a bowie knife she'd stolen from Nicky's wood's stash out of her bra. She smiled menacingly and tossed her head. Renee dug her feet into the dirt, but she was no match for Frankenstein's bride. That's not to say she didn't try. The two women charged each other, Renee protecting her face with her fists. Prescott came slashing like a hell-cat, forcing the knife into her knuckles and twisting.

Renee shrieked as the knife came down through the top of her hand and out the inside of her wrist. Prescott brought her knee up and cracked Renee's chin making her fall backward bleeding and moaning on the ground.

Prescott spun on her heel.

"I've come to save you, Army. We can run away now! Be together always...We'll take Alex and use Dr. Swift's procedure on him. We'll live forever the three of us..."

Army's hair stood on end. He balled his fists up.

"You listen to me, you crazy braud! Bringing you back from the dead was not my idea! The thought of necrophilia makes me want to shoot myself! You stay away from me!" Army was scaling the Datsun's cab. From where she writhed on the ground, Renee realized he hadn't been a willing participant in her resurrection.

Mrs. Prescott tilted her head to the side. She was wan with horror and filled with sudden searing revulsion.

"Necrophilia? I returned from the dead to be with you and this how you talk to me?"

She approached him so agonizingly slow. Renee watched in choiceless suspense. Prescott's fury was not the thing of animals, monsters, or even movies. The look on her face was serenity. Not animosity but love. Love enticed into brutal pain. Pain that lead her to reach out and pull up Army's chains. She broke them in her hands and forced them down his nostrils.

Renee screamed and looked away. She heard Alex's muffled cries of horror and knew that Army's end had been more horrible than she'd ever be able to wrap her mind around.

Prescott broke the chains out of the trunk and began to draw the body away.

"You are going back to Hell with me you son of a-" She never finished the words. Prescott had exerted her newly risen body far too much. Her eyes fluttered in instant vertigo and she collapsed.

It took seconds for Renee to realize she was dead. She kicked Army to roll him over on his belly where she wouldn't have to look at his face.

"Oh my God!" Marilyn had approached the scene. She had clutched Nick under the arms and had dragged him up from the forest. Rabid foam trailed down his neck and his eyes fluttered.

"Alex! What's-what's wrong with?!" He groaned around his gagging.

"You can't say he didn't have it coming, Marilyn. Sometimes life happens to wicked people and brings them to justice. As for the lady, she's happier that way. Whatever they did to her hurt her in ways that could never be fixed." Renee had forced herself to her feet.

Marilyn finally jarred herself into action.

"It's obvious both the boys need saving right? Looks like the medical services around these parts are totally corrupt? What do we do?" Marilyn attempted to think faster than possible. Her heart was beating in the tip of her tongue. She wasn't throwing up only because she'd had nothing to eat for hours.

"We take them to the officers that are busting up the mobile labs. We might have a corrupted hospital staff here in Durango, but it's the only one we've got. A few rifles really do come in handy when you need to force the Doctors of Death to perform emergency care!" Renee made a bee-line for the driver's seat. She'd left the knife protruding through her wrist. Needed to keep it wedged together trapping as much of her blood inside the ribbons of flesh as possible.

Marilyn pushed Nick in the back. She reached and lifted Alex up into his lap. Then she laid Nick against her chest and held both the boys.

"Whoa! Your hand?! Maybe I should drive?"

"Necessity is the mother of invention, eh? I'll drive with my teeth if I got to! Sit tight, shut up and hang onto those boys!" Renee kicked the gas.

CHAPTER 16

"On the ground jokers!" Officer Rogers aimed her Glock 22 for the sky and shot off a round. The research assistants flinched and hit their knees.

Braxton was searching the mobile labs with white plastic gloves.

"You're not going to believe the like of illegal substances they've gotten their hands on! I think I've lost all faith in Capitol Hill." He twirled some burning green powder on the tip of his finger. The Datsun crashed through the trees like a Mustang herd through wildfire and came to a wobbly stop in front of them.

"We need permission to borrow the suspects!" Renee leaped from the driver's seat and threw her hands into the air in a surrender gesture.

"What makes you think we're going to let you do that?" Rogers swayed on her feet with a smug smile.

"Are there any other doctors in Durango that know how to reverse this stuff?" Renee tossed her head indicatively over her shoulder. Marilyn stumbled out of the car with one boy hanging off of either arm. Nicky was spitting up blood along with the foam now. Alex had passed out.

"Oh my God!" Braxton covered his mouth.

Rogers face transformed from brash rookie cop to empathizing parent moved by the sight of the dying kids.

"Alright people, we've got to bust up this crime scene and make way for a backwoods surgery." She started directing traffic with her hands.

"Alright, Rodeo Clowns. Up off the ground! If you don't want me to shoot you, then heed my every word. You're going to fix whatever you broke in these kids."

Rogers shot at the suspects feet to get them to move.

"We can't help that one. The Doctor made the serum to cause rapid apoptosis. He'll be dead in minutes." One of the nurses was defiantly staring at Nick.

"You're going to try or I will shoot you. Seeing as the Law has clearly failed in this situation by actually funding you dirtbags, I'm the only thing that stands between you and getting by with murder." Rogers dumped her brass and reloaded.

The Research assistants stared stupidly at the dying boys.

"We don't know how." Several of them said it at the same time.

Marilyn dropped to her knees in horror. This couldn't be happening.

"My-My blood....Moving faster...More hearts to fail..." Alex had miraculously jarred awake and was talking out of his head.

"What is it, son?" Marilyn turned to look at him. He was beating at his chest.

"The Doc said something about two people...About the vest...It's a performance enhancer, right? That it could make you like a god immune to anything...Even Poison? You could use IVs and hook me and Nicky to this machine..." His head bounced on his chest.

"Oh! I think I know! What he's suggesting is suicide but it might actually work!" The Nurses' eyes glittered as she understood.

"What are you gonna-?" Marilyn's eyes crossed, although she felt like she might understand.

"We've discussed this in some of our organ donor studies. The possibility of healing two test subjects by using our Electro-Organic Cardiac Unit (the machine he's wearing) to pump their blood into one another. They would each be receiving the blood volume of two bodies instead of only one. It's never been tested before and could go horribly wrong. However, with more blood to dissolve the poison and neurotransmission responding from both of them to each other's cells…We might be able to use chemicals to reverse Nick's poisoning and the extra blood volume to stop Alex's cardiac arrest as we gradually unhook him from the machine." The Nurse swallowed obviously terrified now.

"If there's even the slightest possibility that it can save them you'd better get to work!" Chief Riggs demanded suddenly coming on the scene.

The woods around Lake Nighthorse had become an operation room. They all moved like gears in a clock as Time skillfully evaded them. Braxton made the scene sterile like he would do for CSI and the boys were laid in the center of plastic tarps. The mobile lab was broken into and all kinds of bizarre machinery were pulled from it.

"These are what the Prescott Project calls neuro-transmit syndicators." The Nurse began as she pulled out these metallic headbands that looked like something out of Star Trek. She fastened one around each of the boys' heads and then hooked a series of electrodes like a CGI creator down their bodies. Lastly, she pulled out life support lines and needles and pierced them into Nick's heart hooking him into the machine.

"Okay, class is now in session. Assuming that this actually does work and that they have the same blood type, the neuro-transmit syndicator will trigger each boy's brain to send stimulants to each other's neurons. The effect will be that they each receive "double" the commands from the brain for natural function. The natural process of blood coagulation will be signaled in "layers" for each boy causing their individual blood cells to coagulate with each other and form one new blood. The blood pressure will then regulate itself as both of their hearts will be naturally pumping their double-volumed single blood through their bodies. With Nick's rapid unbalanced apoptosis (programmed cell death) there will be twice the neurological activity to have to work through and signal this cellular death. The influence of Alex's unaffected blood will also "confuse" and slow down the spread of the serum. Which will buy time for the poison to expire in potency. With Alex's hyper-tachycardia (extremely too fast heart rate) there will be twice the blood to pump through his heart and the rate will naturally be slowed to its more stable rate." The Nurse rubbed her hands together eager and hopeful.

"Come on, baby!" Marilyn held her breath. This was life or death. Healing or disaster. Renee stood with a compress against her bleeding wrist.

"Come on, Alex!"

The death angel hovered in the air for the third time this year. This time, he would go away empty handed. They all watched for a moment as the Mad Science Nurses monitored medical equipment of the future, watching an EKG that showed the activity of multiple hearts at a time, making a note of how the poison caused some of the electronically operating donated hearts to fail. These lines gradually went flat until the neurologically syndicated braided line alone remained. Alex and Nick's hearts beat in time and their brains worked together, somehow saving each other. Nick stopped foaming at the mouth and the Nurse wiped the bloody spit away. Alex's convulsions slowed until they finally ceased.

One good thing had chosen to come from the dark and twisted research in Durango. They witnessed a medical miracle that night as the two brothers blood flowed intravenously between one another and became one and whole. They began to inject chemicals in Nick that caused hydrolysis to the molecules from his poison. This also affected Alex and allowed for the excess potassium and adrenal fluids in his blood to dissolve until he was regulating under what was normal for their shared blood flow.

The boys passed into a deep and restorative medical coma for around 12 hours. When they woke up, they were totally cured without the faintest cellular or neurological damage. The neuro-syndicator was removed and the boys were left on the IV machine until their blood cells began to "reverse coagulate" as the doctors were calling it. They had separate blood and separate brain functions once again.

It would seem that all was well that had ended well. However, one miracle did not absolve the Prescott research program of its decades of blood-guiltiness. There was one more giant to conquer. The huge ethical question of "unsanctioned resurrection".

CHAPTER 17

"It's okay, son. I've got you." Marilyn smiled as she helped Nick climb the steps to Santa Bianca's.

Renee's wards all stood in a line around the porch smiling in awed silence at Nick. He who had been dead was alive to tell the tale. He was healed of all the mad scientific research that had been done to him.

Alex came wobbling up the stairs behind him, insisting that he didn't need any help. Renee reasoned that Alex was more active because resuscitating must be very draining on the constitution and Nick had done that almost three times.

Sally and Brandon were the first to meet Nick as he came up the stairs. Sally reached out and poked Nick then took two steps back nose twitching nervously. Brandon smiled and reached and hugged him.

"Dude, you're a sight for sore eyes. Well, when you aren't on TV scaring the crap out of the whole City anyway." Brandon laughed and then looked down at Marilyn and Renee.

"The Chief's been here and explained everything to us. It's hard to believe we're all siblings, but it kinda makes sense too." Brandon beamed with pride. He swung out both arms and laced one around Nick's shoulders and one around Alex's.

"The State of Colorado has motioned to transfer all funding for this place to the local government. You guys are going to stay in your home with each other. I'm still going to be your Papa Vierra until you're all 18 and longer if you want." Renee folded her arms and glared at all of them.

"The public disturbance you caused, Nicky, lead to the search warrant and arrest of all the politicians involved on the D.C. end of this crime. All of the Research team is now en route for Federal prison. The Wakers, as we're all affectionately calling the other test victims, are being moved to a private rehabilitation and research facility in the Virgin Islands. If they can't stay in Heaven then ,at least, they'll make the most of here on earth." Marilyn smiled and looked at Nick.

"All's left is for me to go and testify with Chief Riggs in the Federal Courts..." She nodded at Nicky and smiled.

"When all's done...I'm moving here to Durango. Renee's agreed to let me have one of the upstairs rooms and fill it with frilly stuff. We're going to be a family for the first time ever Nicky. I'm finally going to do right by you."

Nick was suddenly tearing up. He attempted to stifle his tears behind his palm.

"What's wrong?" Alex wrapped an arm around his shoulders, deeply upset to see him on the verge of tears.

"No, it's what's right, finally. I never had a family before I came here. Now I have one that makes the Brady Bunch look like an economy car in comparison! Not only that, but I'm alive. I'm not...I'm not even supposed to be alive, you realize?" Nick laughed and shook his head the tears already gone.

Marilyn studied him, weighing the odds of all of this. There were many questions which still needed to be answered. Was the act of resurrecting someone who'd been dead for so long really unethical? If it could be done without prolonged pain and horrible side effects then Marilyn was all for it. Here was her son, the perfect specimen of a bad thing turned to good.

Still when did Science and Society go too far? The road to where they were now was riddled with bodies, blood, pain, and horror. Much of it still remained a mystery.

Marilyn shouldered her bag lost in the questions. There would still no doubt remain a long road before they were all answered. But in the wake of mad science, something had emerged that was beautiful and clean without question. Marilyn smiled watching the symmetrical motions and twin like behavior that Nick and Alex had developed as a result of their "neurological syndication". There would now be advance research into the science of "symbiotic therapy".

As long as people worked together as brothers and sisters for the common right of what was best for all then Science would pursue the right ends. It was possible that love was the only thing strong enough to beat Death. The only thing that could save Society as a whole.

Want to read more exciting stories for FREE?

Join my **V.I.P** List now!

I regularly GIVEAWAY FREE books and SPECIAL DISCOUNTS!

Join my mailing list and be one of thousands we already receiving FREEBIES!

Join by visiting this site:

http://www.ravenspress.com/infinitedreamspubbonus/

Or Scan this QR Code from your smartphone to go the website directly

www.ingramcontent.com/pod-product-compliance
Lightning Source LLC
LaVergne TN
LVHW011300200326
834410LV00007B/339